Pigs Over Boulder

Written and Illustrated by
Kerry Lee MacLean

I ♥ Boulder

On the Spot! Books   Boulder

pssst!
LOOK FOR THE
LOCAL ANIMALS
HIDDEN ON EVERY PAGE.

A is for Boulder Airport.
If you look up at the sky
you might see an airplane
and some piggies flying by!

B is for the Bolder Boulder,
a long, long, long, long race.
You can run it if you want to,
just keep up a good pace.

C is for cottonwoods.

WALDEN PONDS WILDLIFE PRESERVE

Boulder County

GREAT BLUE HERONS

MEOW

ACHOOOO!

C is for the cottonwoods
growing tall and fat.
Their cottonseeds are fuzzy,
just like my silly cat.

D is for deer.

d

Garter snakes

D is for the doe and deer
who come to town to munch.
The flowers are their candy
and the trees are their lunch.

D

d

E is for Easter.

E is for easter at Chautauqua,
and a big bag comes in handy,
'cause hiding in the grass and trees
are eggs and chocolate candy!

F is For Flatirons.

F is for the flatirons
where climbers look like specks.
They hang on ropes like maniacs,
and love to risk their necks!

G is for Canadian geese
who honk, honk, honk all day.
I wonder if they're arguing
about who knows the way.

H is for Humane Society. :h:

HUMANE SOCIETY
of Boulder

-cute
froggies!

VOLUNTEER
at the
Humane
Society.
It's FUN!

DONATION

NAME: Blackie
Free to a good,
loving home.

FREE
FROGS

BULLFROGS

H is for the Humane Society,
where I got my doggies.
They care for lonely animals,
like cats, bats and froggies.

I is for ice climbing
up the face of Boulder Falls.
Wear the right equipment
or you'll be sliding down its walls!

J is for joggers.

J is for the joggers
running up and down our streets.
They're burning off the calories
from Chocolate Factory's treats!

K is for kayaking. :b

K is for kayaking
down icy Boulder Creek.
Don't forget your helmet.
And try *not* to spring a leak!

L is for library. :!

L is for the library
where there's a lot to do.
You can borrow books on bugs
and how to make blue goo.

M is for mountain lion.

Grandrabbit's
TOY SHOPPE

ROAR!

ANTS

M is for the mountain lion's
fierce and mighty roar.
But you can hug a gentle one
at Grandrabbit's store.

N is for NCAR

N is for NCAR
where scientists watch the weather.
Go with a friend or two,
discover it together.

O is for owl.

BOBOLINK TRAIL

LOVE
Your World

COYOTES

O is for the Great Horned Owl
whose pellets dot our trails.
Crack one up to see the bones
and rats teeth, *sharp as nails!*

P is for Pearl Street Mall.

P is for Pearl Street
where strolling down the mall
you might see musicians
and a juggler on a ball.

Q is for queen bees.

FRESH HONEY

N. BROADWAY

OUCH!

COLORADO CLOVER HONEY $5.00 jar

RACCOONS

Q is for queen bees,
their workers make all the honey.
Careful not to bother them
it wouldn't be that funny!

R is for red-tailed hawks.

Boulder

WOW!

SCO...
CARPE...
PARK

WOODPECKERS

R is for red-tailed hawks,
dozens live here, too.
You can spot one right in Boulder,
as it's spotting you!

S is for skiing.

BLACK BEARS

S is for skiing.
We slide down the slopes with glee
and think we are *so* elegant
until we hit a tree!

T is for Boulder Theater
where you can see a play.
Parents like to go at night,
but kids go in the day.

U is for university,
where we get an education.
We always throw our hats up high
right after graduation.

V is for violin concerts.

HAUTAUQUA PARK

Big-eared bats

V is for violins
playing at Chautauqua.
We dance as the sun sets,
purple, pink, and aqua.

W is for watersports.

W is for water sports,
this one's a disgrace.
We drag ourselves through mud and call it
the kinetic race!

X is for x-rays.
We play every sport that's known.
With all this healthy living,
someone's bound to break a bone!

Y is for yuletide.

Y is for yuletide,
when all of Boulder dreams
of fast boats, new dollies,
and chocolate buttercreams.

Z is for zoomers. Z

Z is for Zoomers,
zooming fast on bikes.
They whiz past us bladers
like whirlwinds, oh *yikes!*

Published by On the Spot! Books
1492 Tipperary Street
Boulder, CO 80303

ISBN 0-9652998-0-5

Printed in Hong Kong

The pictures in this book were painted in acrylic.

PIGS OVER BOULDER

**Help your child get an overview of Boulder and show them where our
local animals really live. Ask your book dealer about our new poster, the
PIGS OVER BOULDER MAP.**

TO HECTOR, LELAND, SPECIAL THANKS TO AMY NICOLSON, KELLY, ANDREW, SOPHIE, GREGORY, TESSA AND KELLY. LINDA, MARK, PHYLLIS, CAYLA, SANDY, + NANCY'S CLASS